The Last Wolf
of Humphrey Head

Andrew Musgrave

ISBN: 978-0-9955868-5-7

Lightship Guides and Publications
(lightshipguides@gmail.com)

All text and illustrations are by the author.

Thanks to Leon, to Alastair, to Vir and to John,
to Woodie & Rosie, Gary, & Peter,
& to Miggie (courtesy of Glenis)
for your assistance with re-enactments.

Lightship Guides & Publications

In the south tip of the English Lake District is an area of land that projects into Morecambe Bay called the Cartmel Peninsula, where for hundreds of years **the legend of the Last Wolf** has survived.

Here, on the west flank of Humphrey Head, is an arch in the limestone cliffs guarding the entrance to a small cave and where, allegedly, the last wolf in all of England had its lair.

But this wolf was killing the flocks of sheep of the farmers who lived in the area.

So, **Sir Edgar Harrington**, who lived nearby at **Wraysholme Tower**, suggested a competition to be rid of this last wolf. He offered half his estate, and the hand of his niece in marriage, to the knight who could kill the annoying beast.

All this supposedly took place in the 13th / 14th century, almost eight hundred years ago.

Later, an anonymous poet wrote a ballad about the legend, called *The Last Wolf: a Legend of Humphrey Head*. (Some credit Edwin Waugh as the poet since he mentions it in a journal in 1861).

Then in 1906, Mrs Jerome Mercier wrote down the story in a little book called *The Last Wolf*. This book is now out-of-print, but a copy can still be obtained from local libraries, and some second-hand copies are available on-line.

This book is my own version of the legend. The Cumbrian locations and medieval costumes are authentic, but I have taken the liberty of slightly changing the ending. I hope you enjoy my little tale and find it amusing...

Andrew Musgrave, January 2020

The Last Wolf

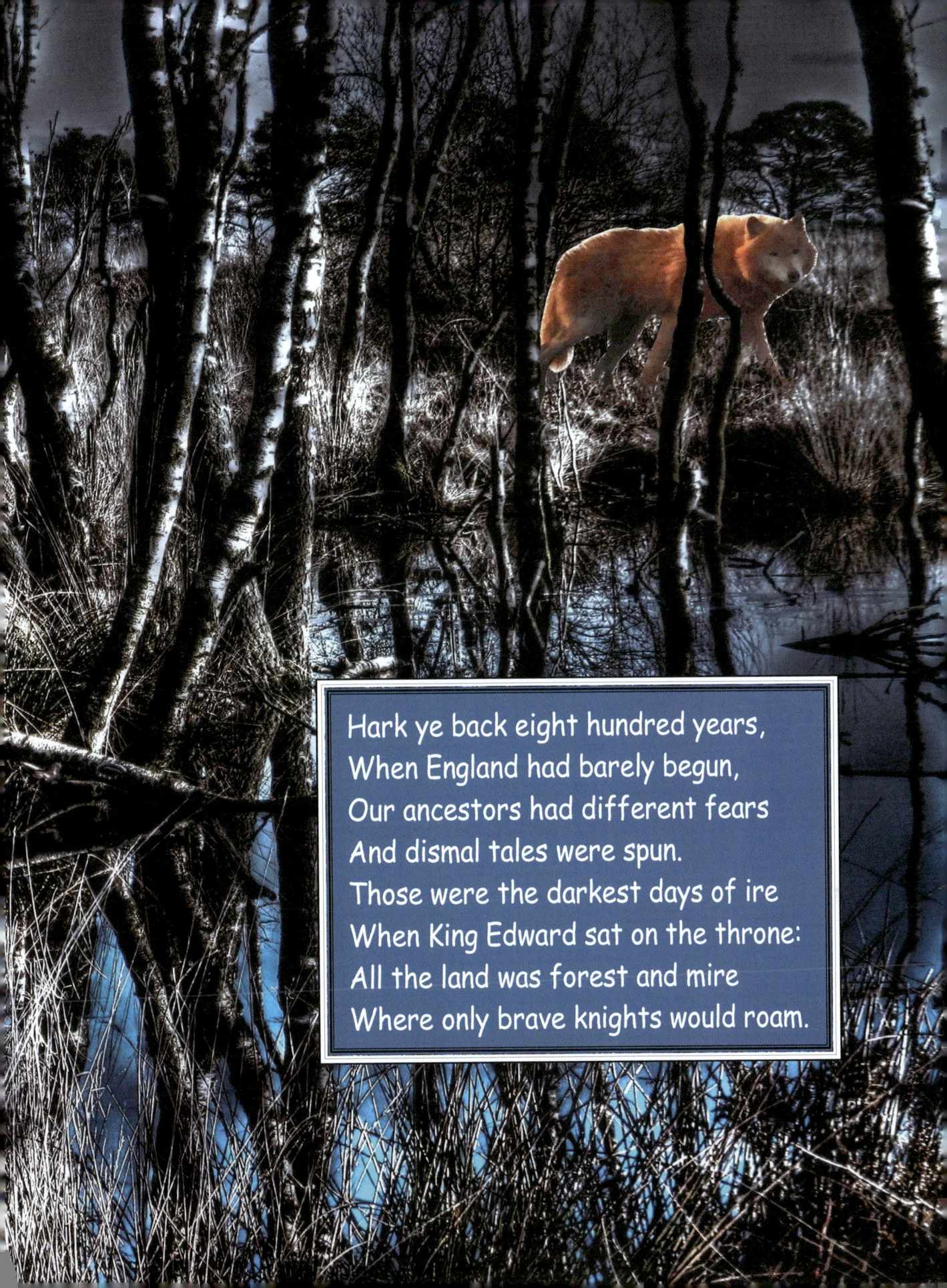

Hark ye back eight hundred years,
When England had barely begun,
Our ancestors had different fears
And dismal tales were spun.
Those were the darkest days of ire
When King Edward sat on the throne:
All the land was forest and mire
Where only brave knights would roam.

Celts ploughed the land and tended the shoots
On the soil strewn with Roman pots,
The folk on the strand had Viking roots
Fearing raids from the northern Scots.
'Twas here amidst yew and pine and birch
Where red deer came to wallow,
Some monks chose a spot for their sacred church
In Cartmel's lake-strewn hollow.

Not far away near Humphrey's Head
Where monks strew their nets in the creek
Lived a man and his son and his pretty niece, fed
From the milk of the earth so bleak.
But by strain and stealth they grew in wealth
And improved on their little bower,
They created a home where the sheep hogs roam
And they called it WRAYSHOLME TOWER.

Kirkhead looms like a humpbacked whale
Scouring for the tides,
Beneath its flanks in the wooded ranks
Is where the LAST OF THE WOLVES resides,
Eyeing its prey at the dusk of day,
Unseen in its dappled hide:
The ewes that graze and the hog that strays
Add to the toll that died.

The lord of the land near Allithwaite's strand
Sees the carcasses strewn in the field;
Where the wolf ran amok destroying his flock
The evidence is clearly revealed.
Shouting his curse (and other things worse),
With vengeance his soul is instilled,
Ere it costs him his life he must end this strife:
He vows THAT WOLF MUST BE KILLED!

Now, this lord of the manor of Wraysholme –
SIR EDGAR was his name –
Had a tendency to make folks dislike him,
What with his burly, bullying frame;
All grumpy, gruff, and grim,
He was certainly someone to fear –
Though a few found him slightly amenable
When plied with mead and with beer –
But the consensus among serfs and villeins,
Who were ignorant loyal folk
Agreed he was merely a scoundrel,
A rascally roguish bloke.

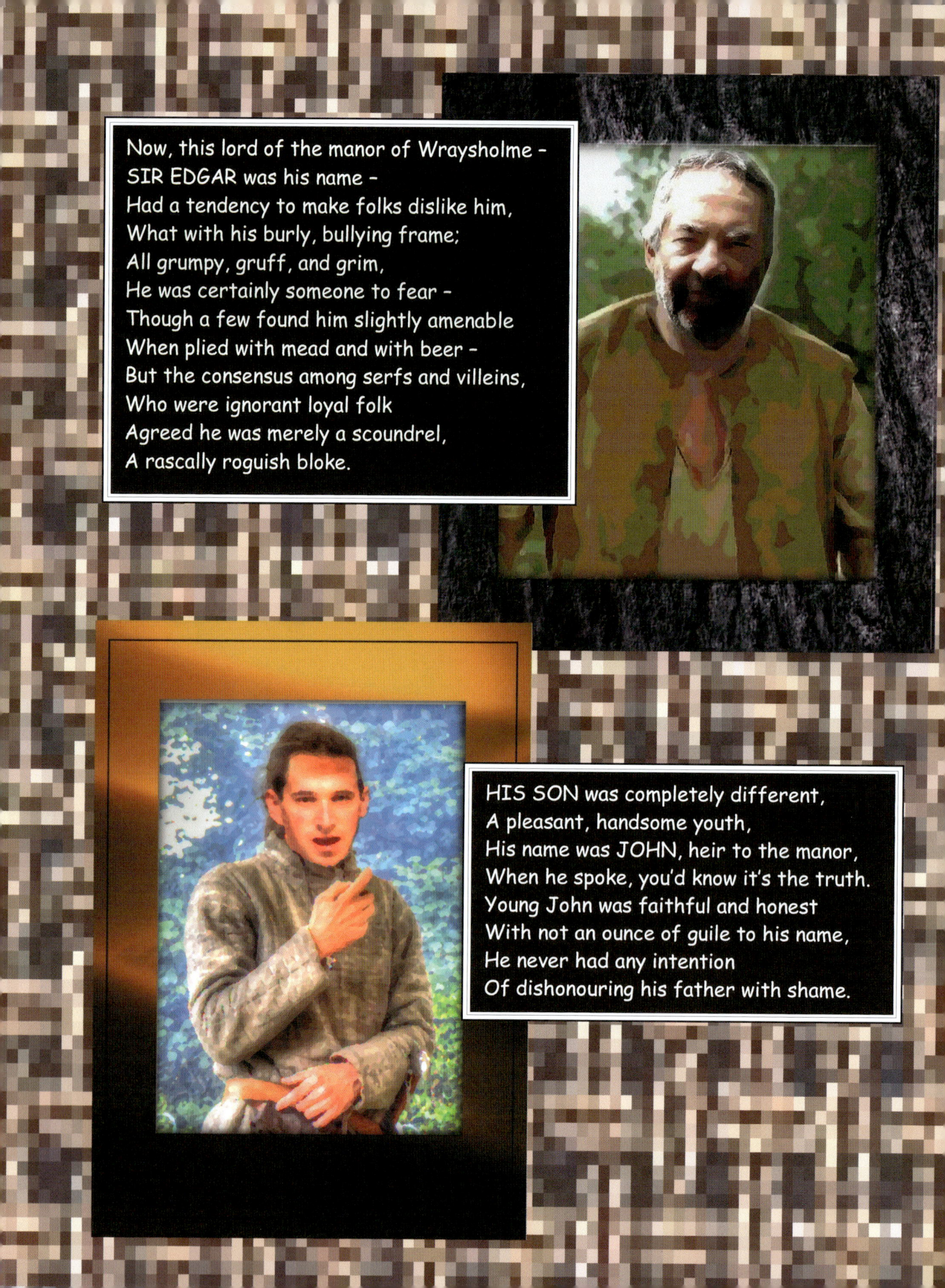

HIS SON was completely different,
A pleasant, handsome youth,
His name was JOHN, heir to the manor,
When he spoke, you'd know it's the truth.
Young John was faithful and honest
With not an ounce of guile to his name,
He never had any intention
Of dishonouring his father with shame.

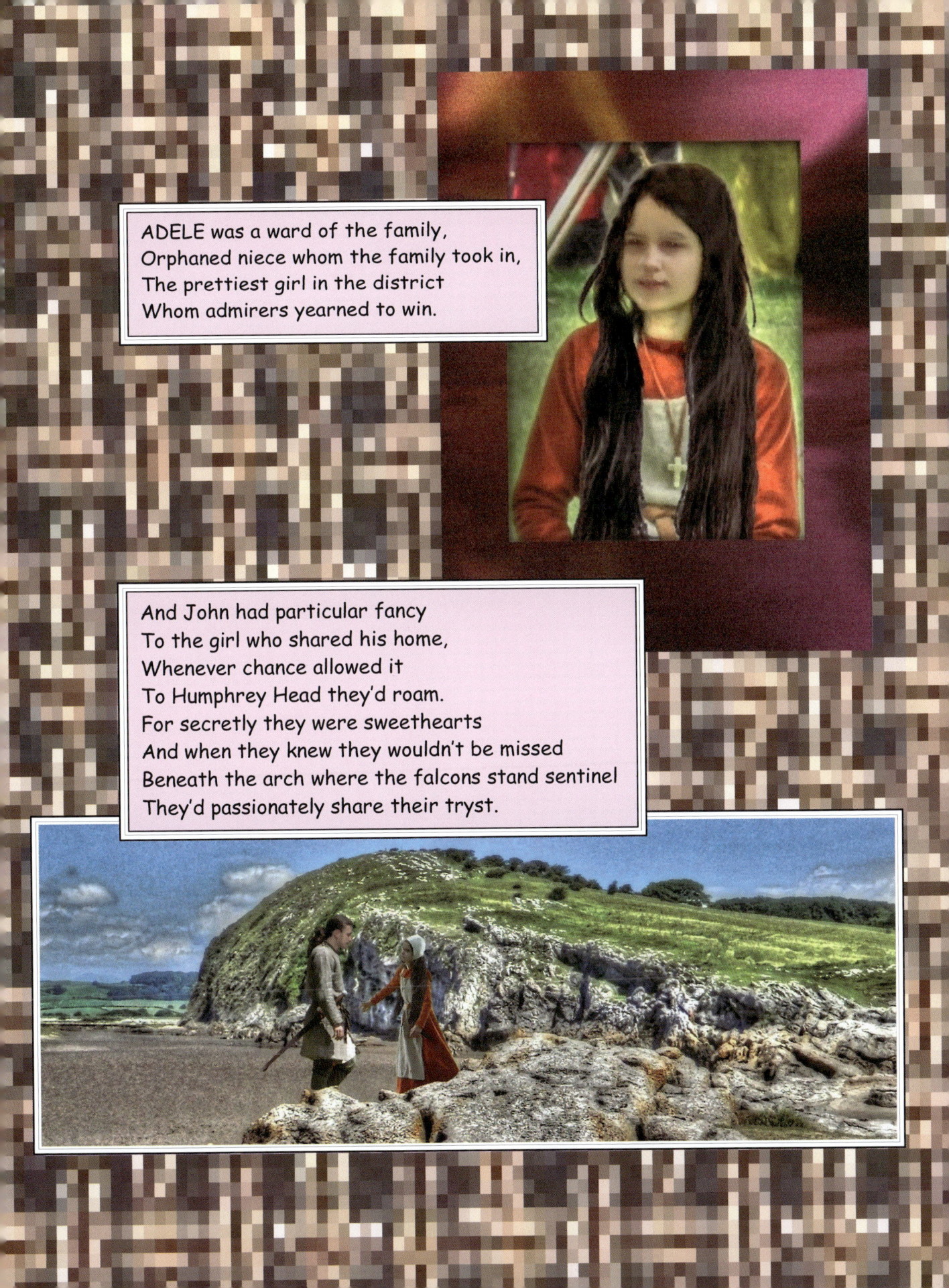

ADELE was a ward of the family,
Orphaned niece whom the family took in,
The prettiest girl in the district
Whom admirers yearned to win.

And John had particular fancy
To the girl who shared his home,
Whenever chance allowed it
To Humphrey Head they'd roam.
For secretly they were sweethearts
And when they knew they wouldn't be missed
Beneath the arch where the falcons stand sentinel
They'd passionately share their tryst.

Now, back to the blackguard Sir Edgar,
Wraysholme's deviant boss:
He'd thought of a way to replenish,
To make up for his wolf-ravished loss.
'We'll wait till darkness envelopes,
And creep to the village of Cark,
While their shepherds are somnolently sleeping,
We'll rustle their flocks in the dark.'

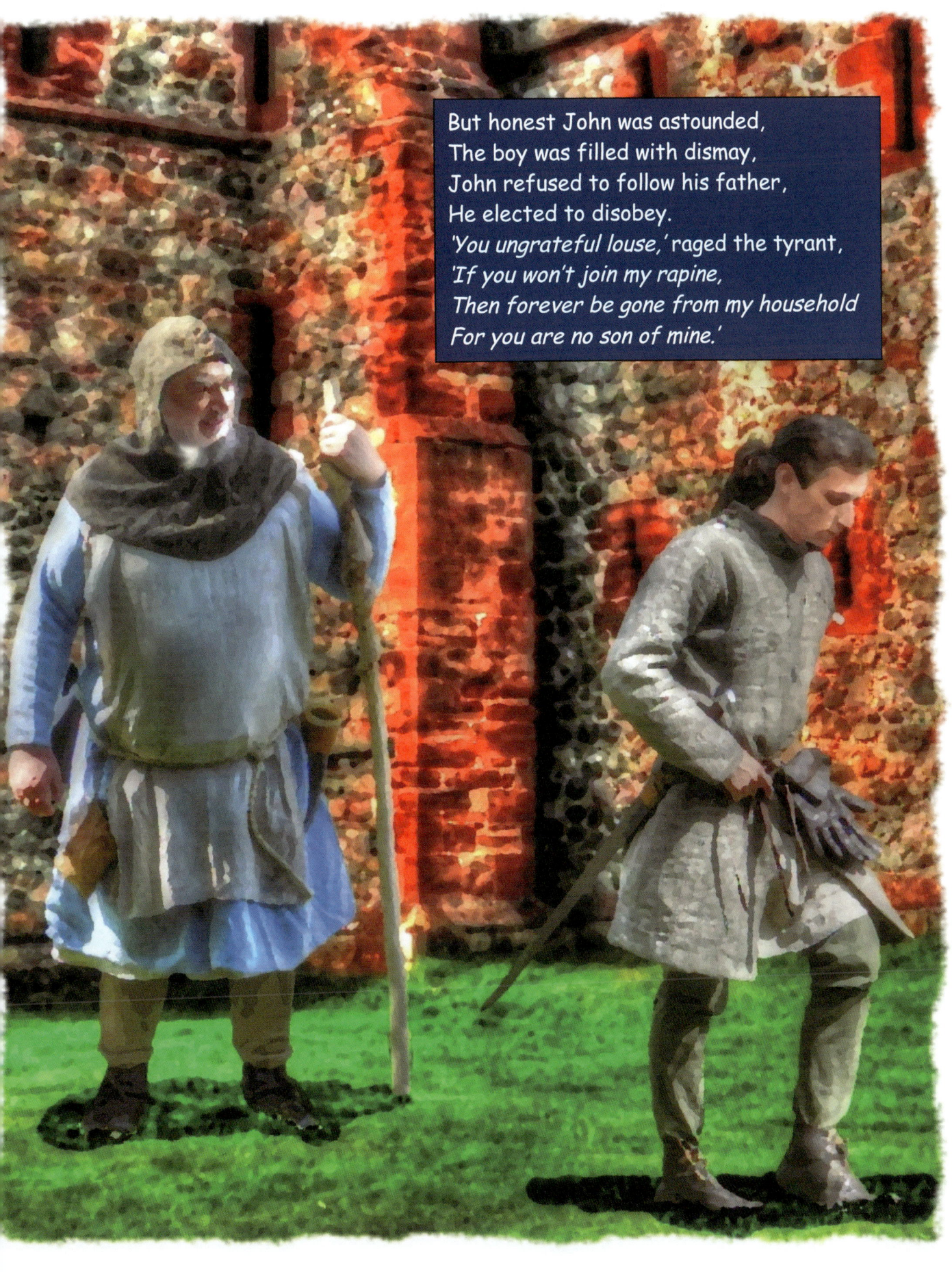

But honest John was astounded,
The boy was filled with dismay,
John refused to follow his father,
He elected to disobey.
'You ungrateful louse,' raged the tyrant,
'If you won't join my rapine,
Then forever be gone from my household
For you are no son of mine.'

So with sorrow John fled from his father,
He departed heavy of heart,
He knew that now and forever
From his cousin he'd be apart.
'For all that Wraysholme has brought me
I'd rather sink into hell,
For all that honesty's taught me
I won't betray the trust of Adele.'

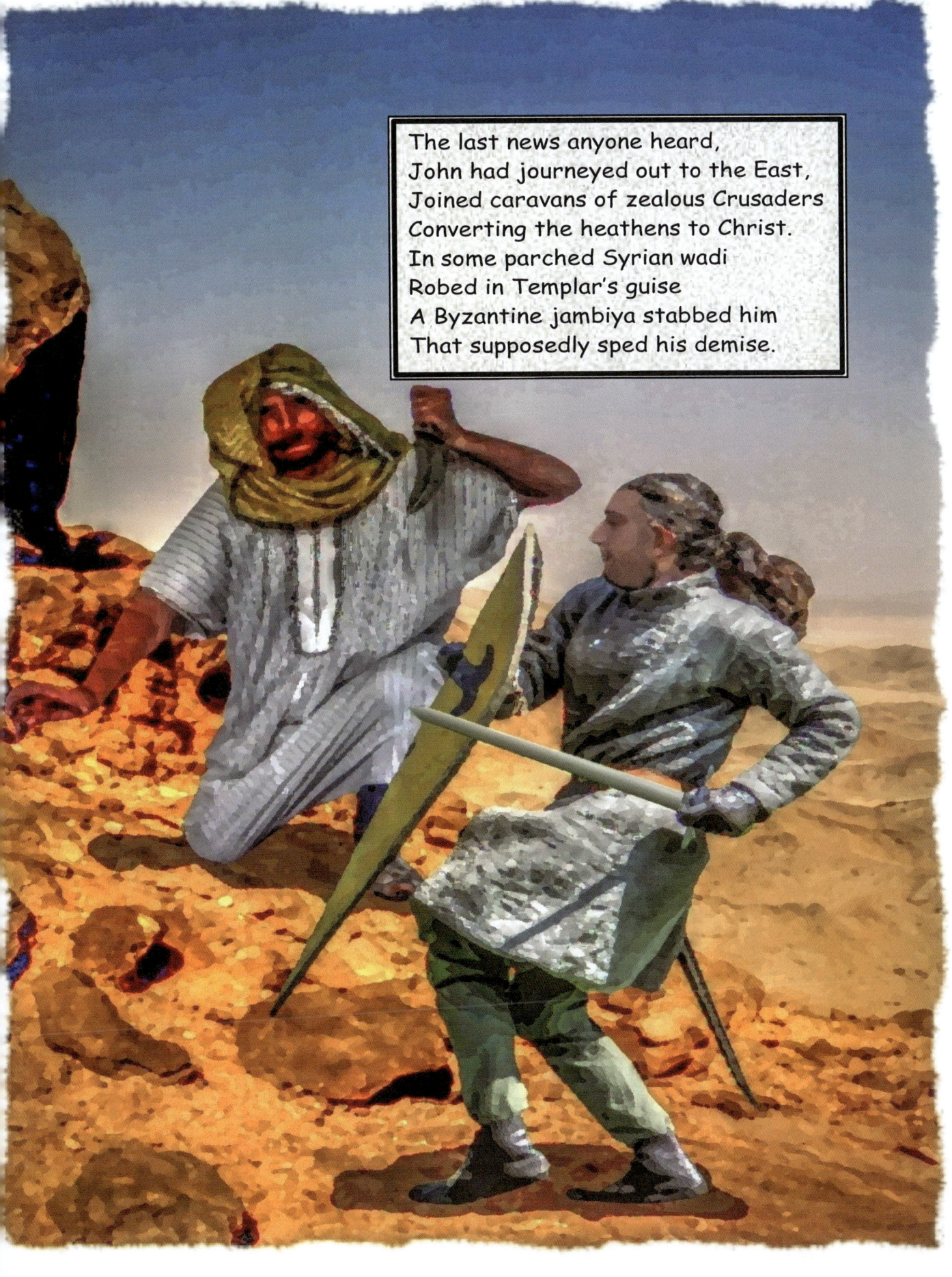

The last news anyone heard,
John had journeyed out to the East,
Joined caravans of zealous Crusaders
Converting the heathens to Christ.
In some parched Syrian wadi
Robed in Templar's guise
A Byzantine jambiya stabbed him
That supposedly sped his demise.

And so Sir Edgar Harrington,
Despite the illusive wolf's stealth,
Through indulgence lost his only son,
Yet managed to amass lordly wealth.

As each day
went by
Lord Edgar filled all
with dread.

As weeks passed young
John seemed ever
more dead.

As months crawled on the wolf grew ever more cunning.

As years progressed Adele grew ever more stunning!

For the knight who can prove
the wolf is slain
I'll grant him the gift
of half my domain.
To the knight who brings me
the slain wolf's head
To my niece Adele
he shall be wed. "

The proclamation went out to far and wide
To win the prize of that pretty bride,
Many a knight hoped that wolf to slay
Girding their loins for that promised day.

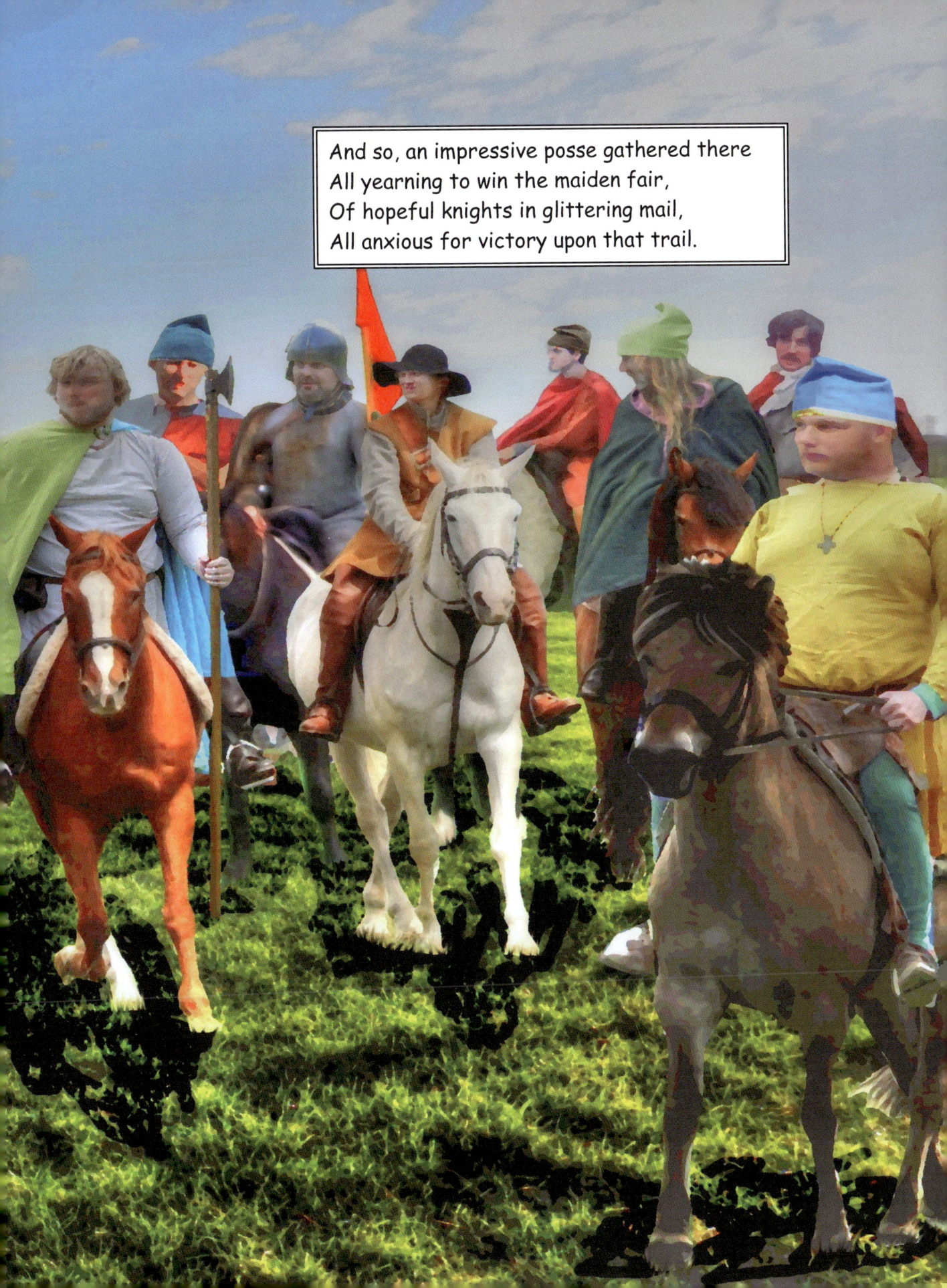

And so, an impressive posse gathered there
All yearning to win the maiden fair,
Of hopeful knights in glittering mail,
All anxious for victory upon that trail.

Assembled there with the strength of seven
Was Sir Matthew Redeman from the hall at Leven.

On his sturdy steed
looking ready and tough
Was the imposing figure
of Vipont from Brough.

Each serf and soul
would be sure to cower
When confronted by Dallam
from Arnside's Tower.

Dressed with his finest
embroidered tassle
Was Robert Stirkeland
of Sizergh Castle.

Could you conceive your chances were even
If you met Sir Musegros of Kirkby Stephen?

Any stray wolf need watch it fang
When Wharton pursues it from Mallerstang,

And any bold wolf need guard its hide
When stalked in its tracks by John Burneside.

With Sir Lancelot Threlkeld out to pursue
There was Muncaster, Lowther and Leyburne, too.

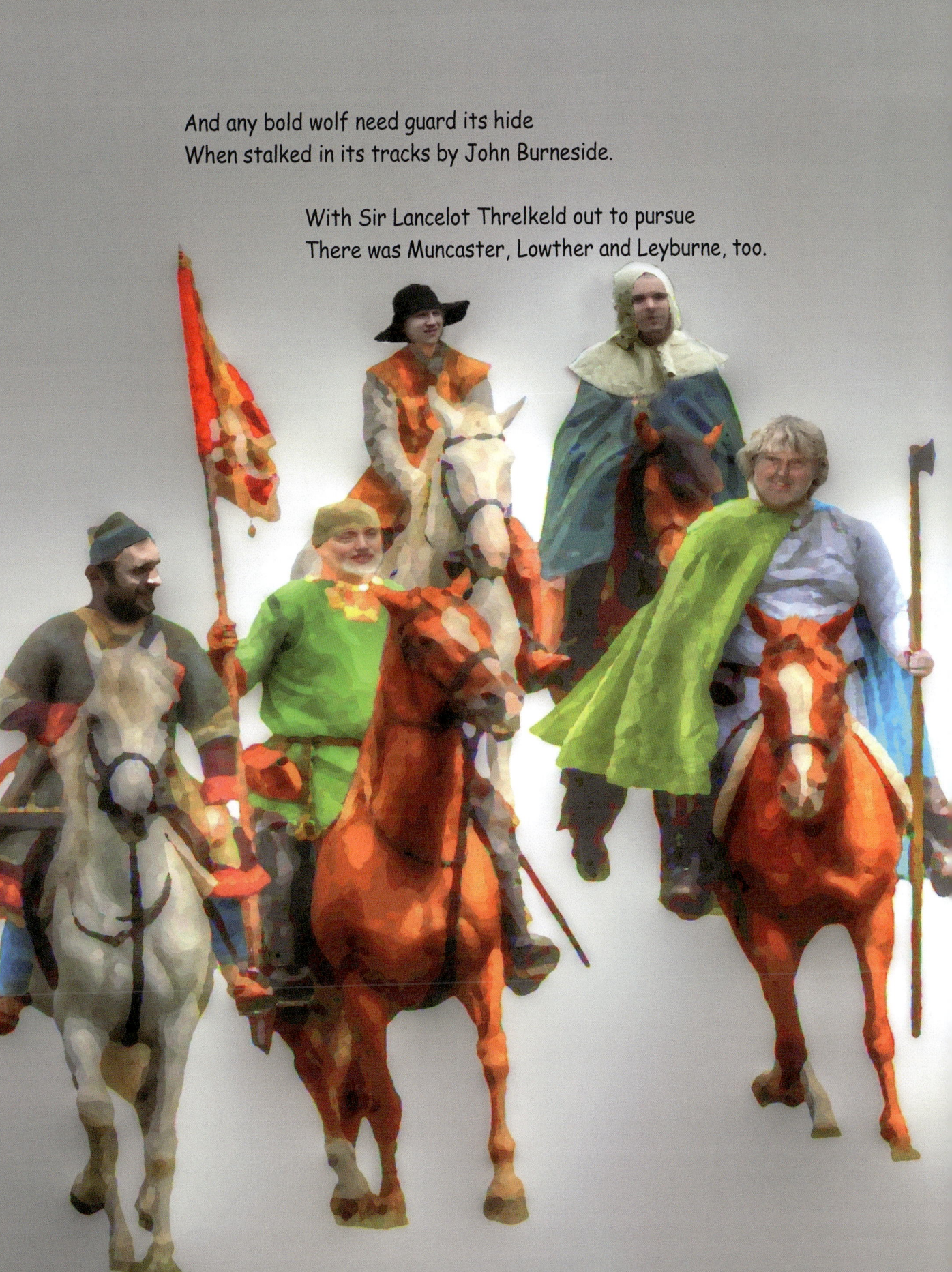

All were eager for the race to start,
All had that maiden stamped on their heart,
All yearned for victory in the race to win
And wrench that wolf from its sinuous skin.

But wait, one knight rides from the south instead,
Emerging from the sands round Humphrey's Head,
Alone across the treacherous bay he's ridden,
A mysterious knight with his face kept hidden.
As his mud-caked horse strains from that perilous defile,
He mumbles his name as 'John de L'isle'.

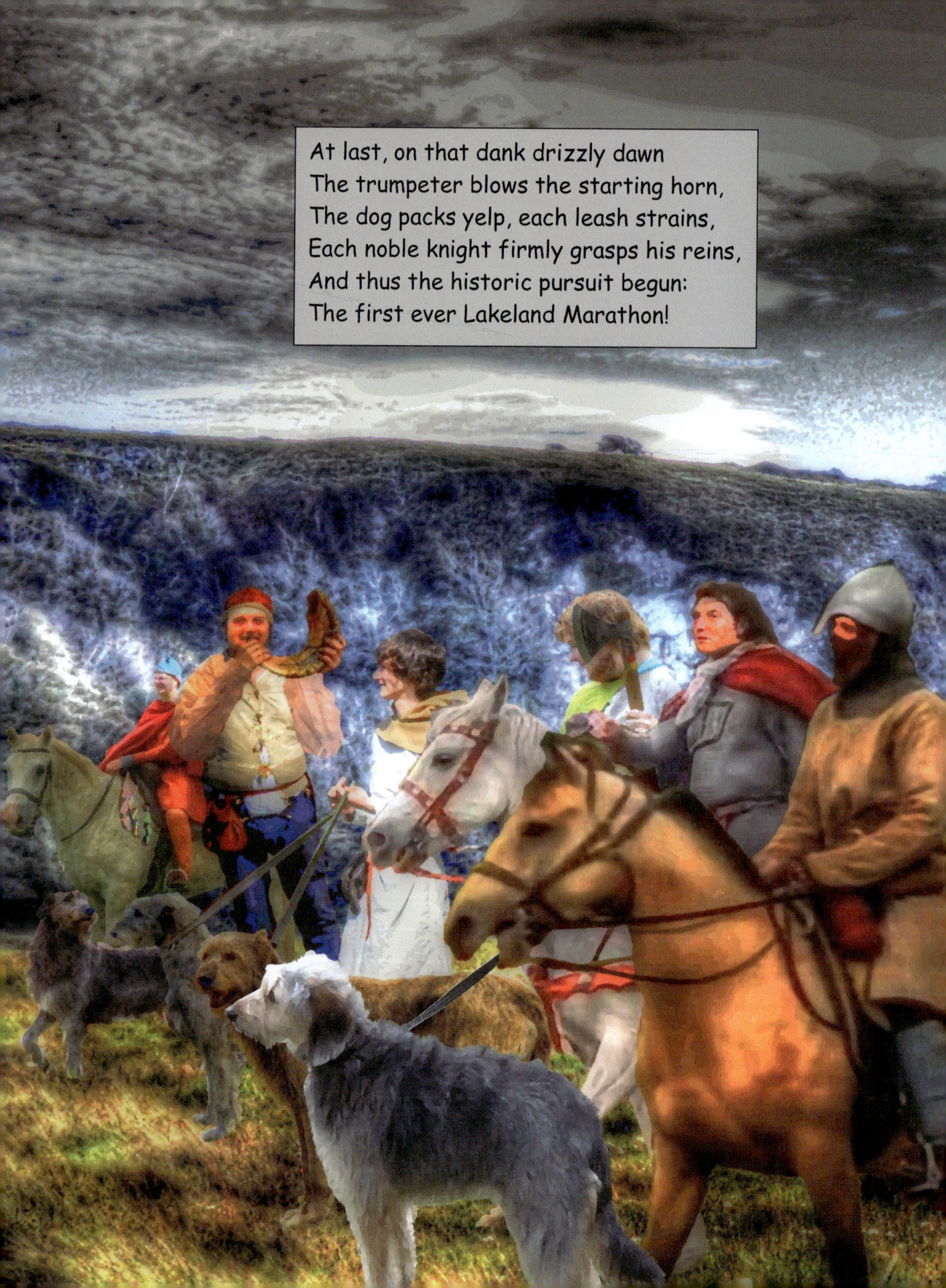

At last, on that dank drizzly dawn
The trumpeter blows the starting horn,
The dog packs yelp, each leash strains,
Each noble knight firmly grasps his reins,
And thus the historic pursuit begun:
The first ever Lakeland Marathon!

Sir Edgar wished them luck and godsend,
He knew e'er nightfall his troubles would end;
Lady Adele mouthed a fearful confession,
By day's end, she'd be some stranger's possession.

Full of bravado the posse planned to scare
That monstrous beast from out its lair,
The naïve among them even had a hunch
The job would be finished well before lunch.

But the wolf had already escaped this noose
It was out on the fells carefree and loose,
Mysteriously, John knew the route it would follow:
Up Barnard's Mount and onto How Barrow.

Below, de L'Isle could see monks till and toil
The saturated sods of Cartmel's soil,
To the west, quicksands in the estuary
Could ensnare a soul wading carelessly.

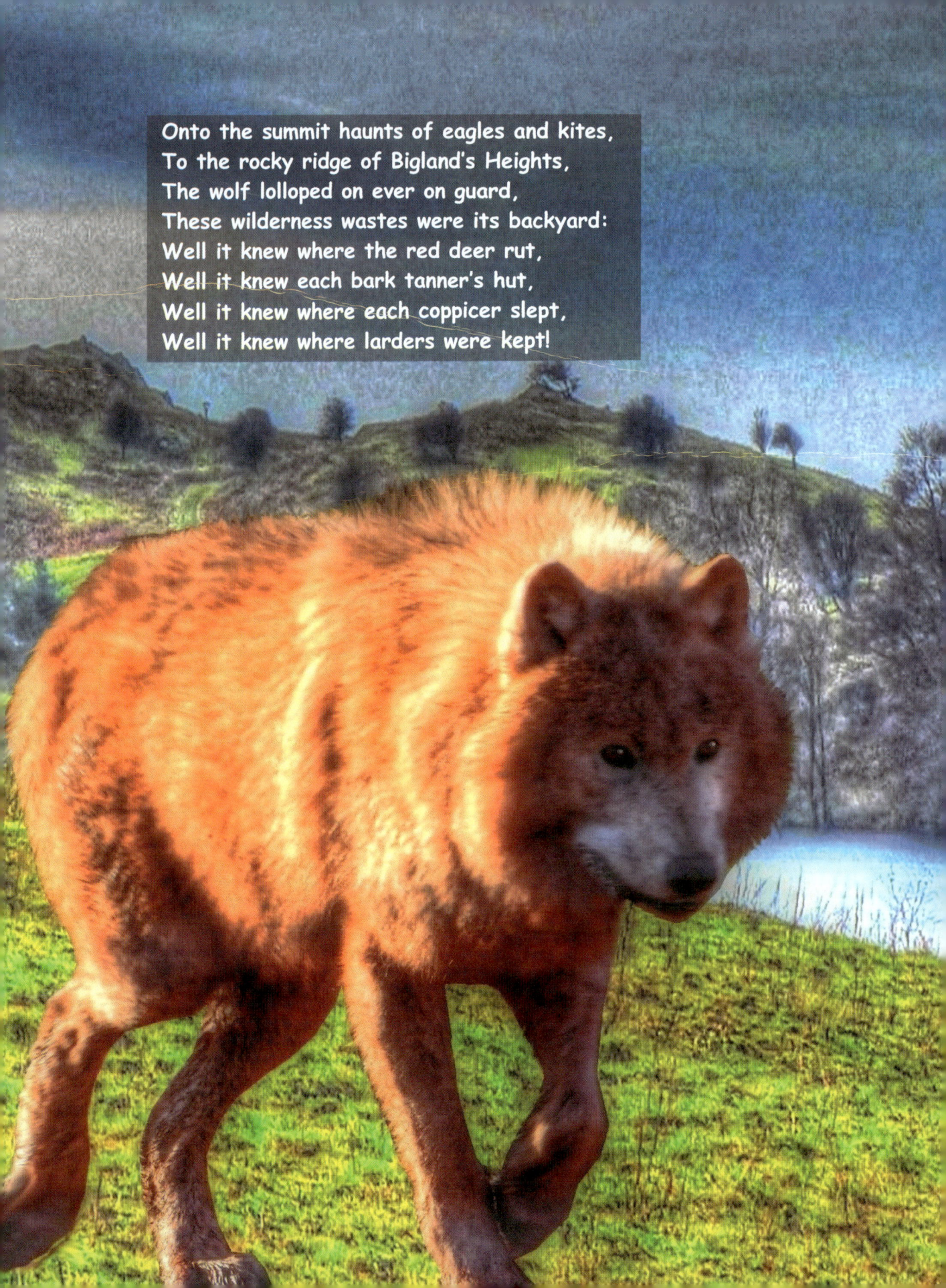

Onto the summit haunts of eagles and kites,
To the rocky ridge of Bigland's Heights,
The wolf lolloped on ever on guard,
These wilderness wastes were its backyard:
Well it knew where the red deer rut,
Well it knew each bark tanner's hut,
Well it knew where each coppicer slept,
Well it knew where larders were kept!

The wolf bounded down o'er Fish House mire,
It would be fatal now if it started to tire,
It feared being impaled by a knight's cold blade
As across the Leven it started to wade,
It feared an ending lethal and cruel
As it frantically swam across Rusland Pool.

But ahead of the chasing mob it stayed
As hounds and horses yelped and brayed,
The pursuit raced on at a fearful rate
As the wolf led the chase to the lake at Nibthwaite.

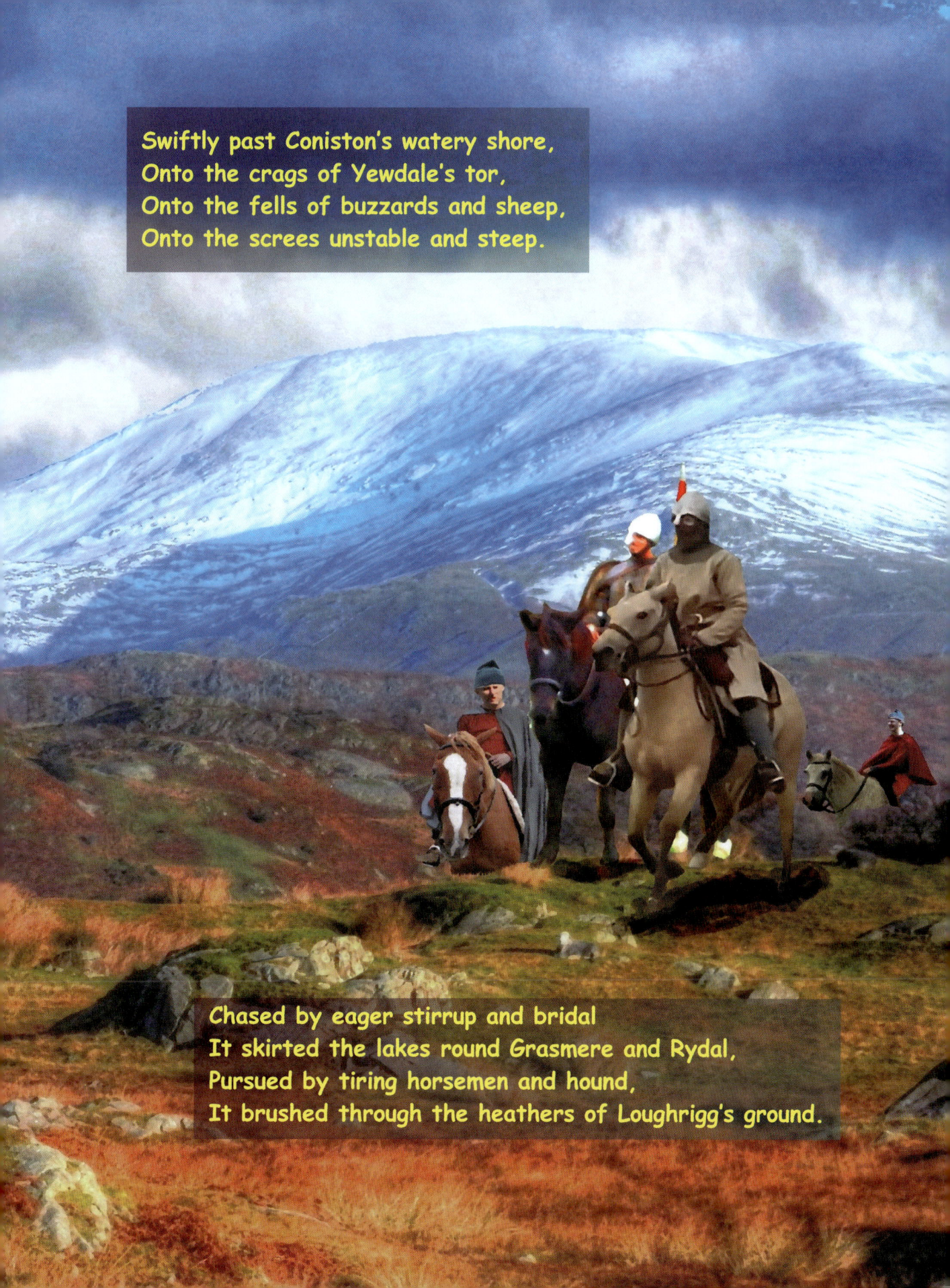

Swiftly past Coniston's watery shore,
Onto the crags of Yewdale's tor,
Onto the fells of buzzards and sheep,
Onto the screes unstable and steep.

Chased by eager stirrup and bridal
It skirted the lakes round Grasmere and Rydal,
Pursued by tiring horsemen and hound,
It brushed through the heathers of Loughrigg's ground.

All day long the race ensued,
All day long the chasers pursued,
Till one by one
   hounds fell off the pace,
And one by one
   knights tired of the chase.

Redeman was first
   to curtail his ramble
When his horse got ensnared
   in thorny bramble,

And Stirkeland was forced to early retire
Getting bogged down in Brathay mire,

Musegros reluctantly relinquished his goal
Struggling up Latterbarrow's craggy knoll,

And Wharton gave up his dubious claim
Once his dappled grey horse became tired and lame.

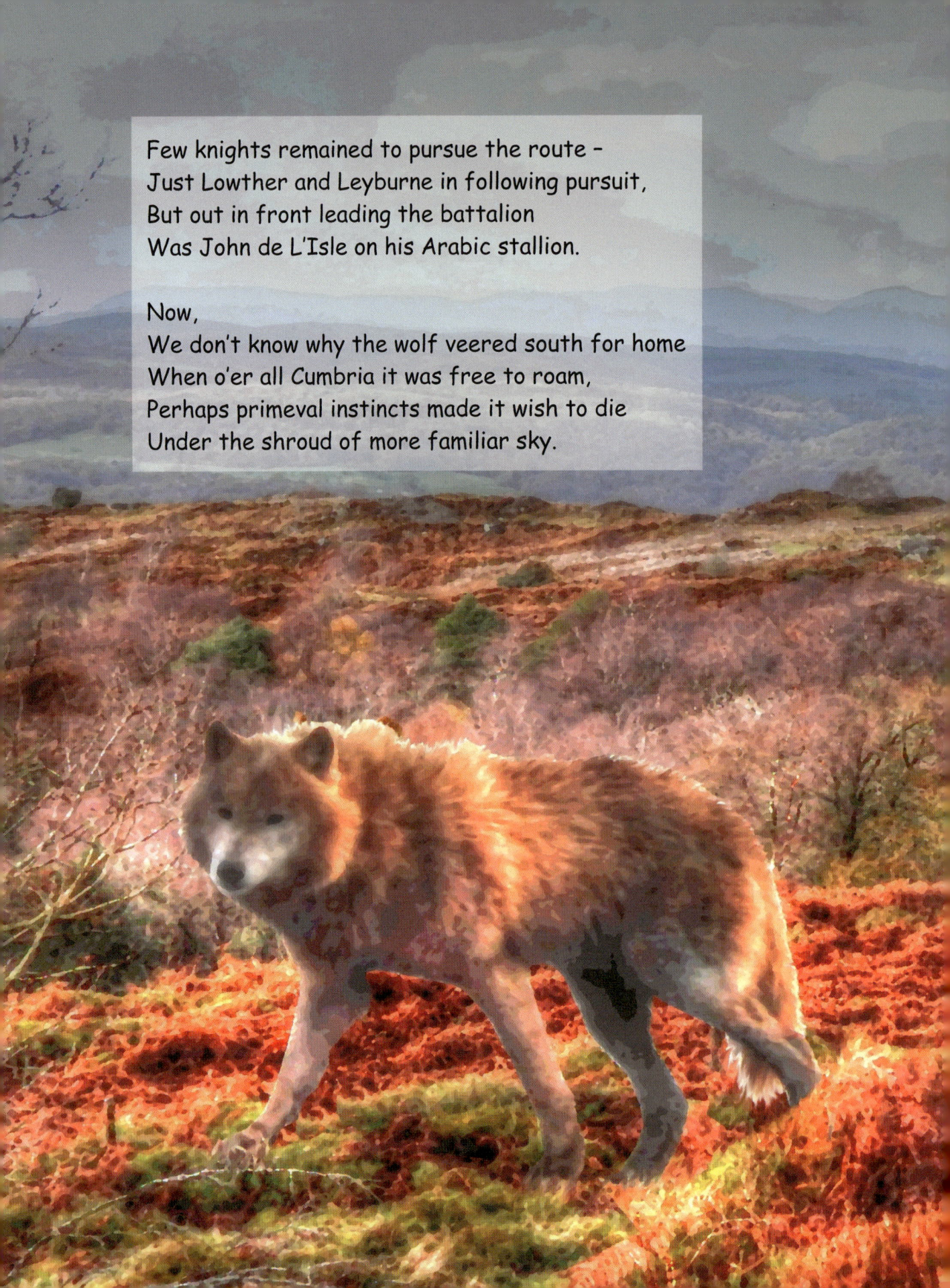

Few knights remained to pursue the route –
Just Lowther and Leyburne in following pursuit,
But out in front leading the battalion
Was John de L'Isle on his Arabic stallion.

Now,
We don't know why the wolf veered south for home
When o'er all Cumbria it was free to roam,
Perhaps primeval instincts made it wish to die
Under the shroud of more familiar sky.

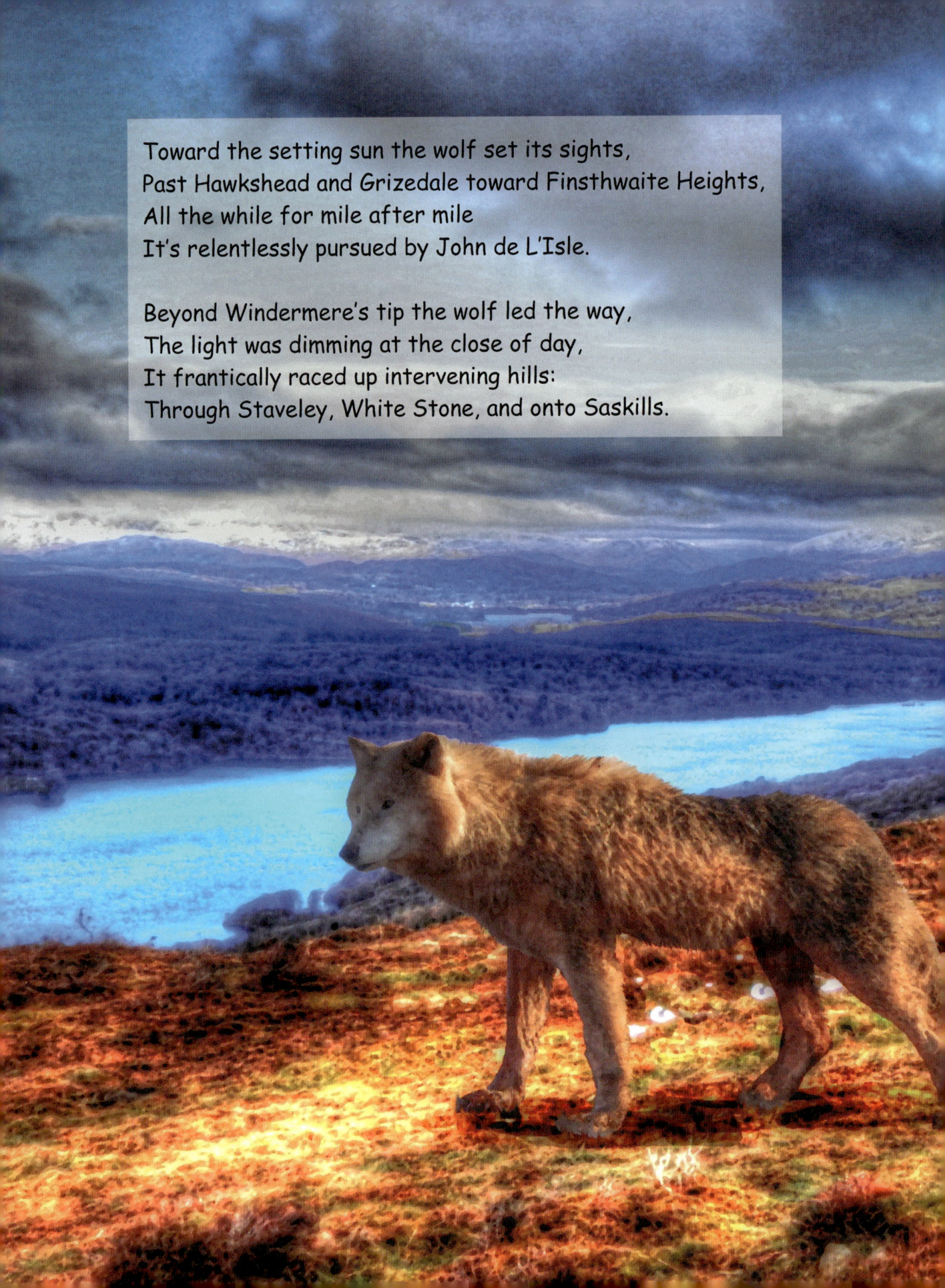

Toward the setting sun the wolf set its sights,
Past Hawkshead and Grizedale toward Finsthwaite Heights,
All the while for mile after mile
It's relentlessly pursued by John de L'Isle.

Beyond Windermere's tip the wolf led the way,
The light was dimming at the close of day,
It frantically raced up intervening hills:
Through Staveley, White Stone, and onto Saskills.

At last the wolf spied familiar turf,
It could sense the scent of seafoam and surf,
It could see in the gloom a few miles ahead
The whaleback form of Humphrey Head.

But like a nagging wasp
one can never evade
De L'Isle on his trail
forever stayed,
Like a restless vulture
circles the sky,
Instinctively the wolf
Knew its time to die.

The wolf chose to make its final stand
Near the marshy shores of Flookburgh's strand,
On the sheep-cropped turf of ling and heath
Is where it would bravely bare its teeth,
On the sheer lime cliffs where ivy hangs
Is where it will display its powerful fangs,
On the windswept ridge where elder grows bent
Is where its pursuers will be fatally rent.

An arch marks the entrance to cave and lair
Where stood the last wolf in its final dare,
John de L'Isle arrives with daggers drawn
Confronting the beast standing forlorn.

Did you hear the final howl
  as it solemnly faced death?
Could you smell the rotting scent
  from its rancid dying breath?
Did you feel the heavy thud
  as it collapsed on quivering knees?
Could you see its tangled mane
  wrangled by the breeze?

Why no!
John is not motivated by a needless blood lust.
De L'Isle is not content to make a murderous thrust,
The knight doesn't lunge with his cold steel spear.
Instead crusader boldly draws near.
Bafflingly, man and wolf start to debate,
He offers a parley to seal the wolf's fate,
It is not inevitable that a beast should die,
Both can live happily beneath the same sky,

'I've not chased round Cumbria your life to rob:
Instead, I'm offering you a special job!
Become a guardian wolf to <u>*protect*</u> *our flocks,*
Keep other predators from stealing our stocks.
You'll get a generous portion of steak each day
If you successfully keep rustlers at bay.'

Man and wolf in full harmony
Mutually decided it's best to agree,
The wolf cur agreed, as it settled its fur:
(And that's what it means when we say *we concur*!)

And so...
Stately John rode, his wolf by his side,
A conquering crusader, a winner with pride,
In full sight of all he removed his disguise,
Rode up to his father to claim his prize.

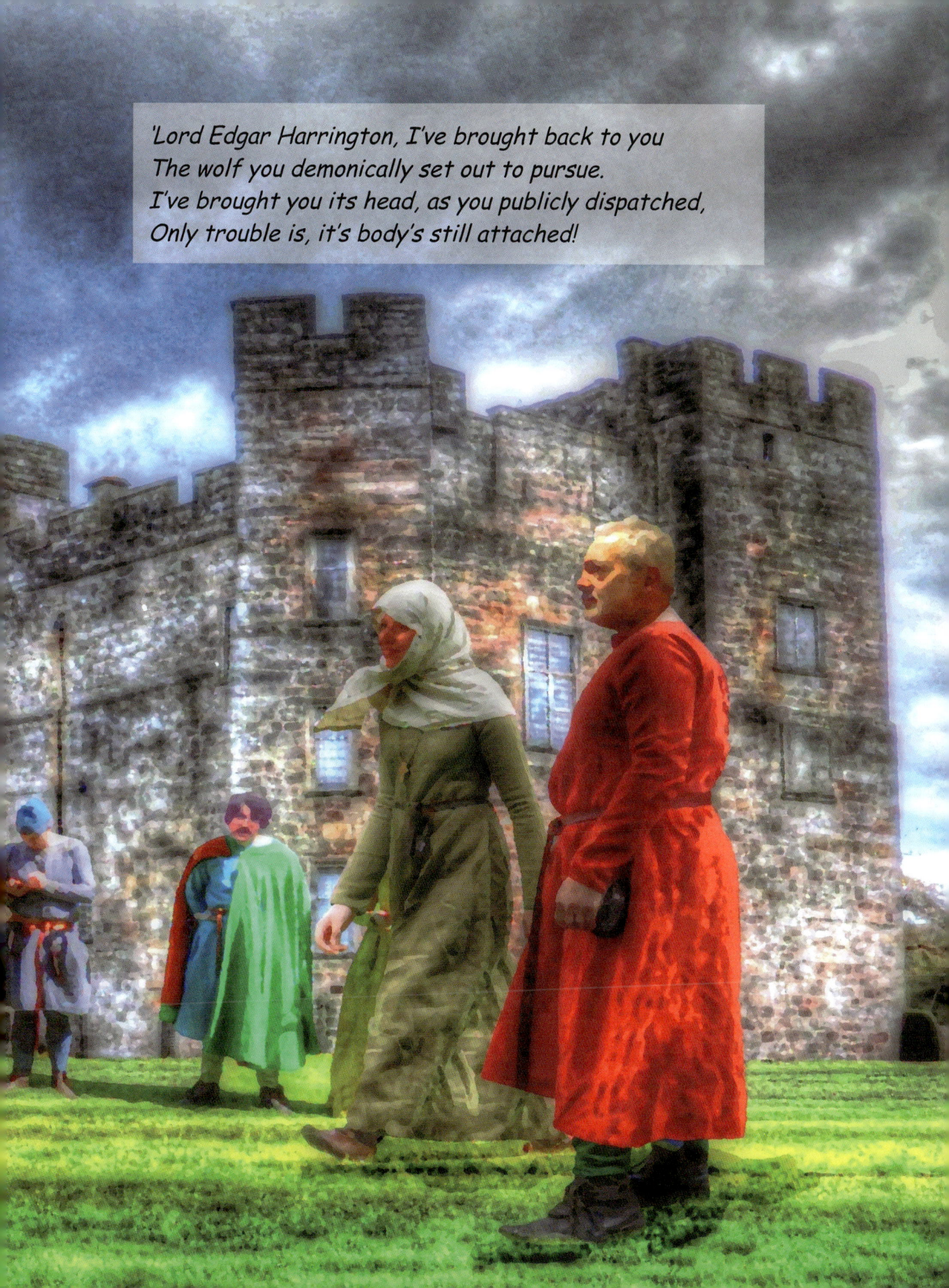

'Lord Edgar Harrington, I've brought back to you
The wolf you demonically set out to pursue.
I've brought you its head, as you publicly dispatched,
Only trouble is, it's body's still attached!

'The reward I seek from winning this ride
Is that my sweetheart, Adele, shall be my bride,
This wolf will be trained our sheep to guard,
And this wolf will be tamed like a dog in the yard.'

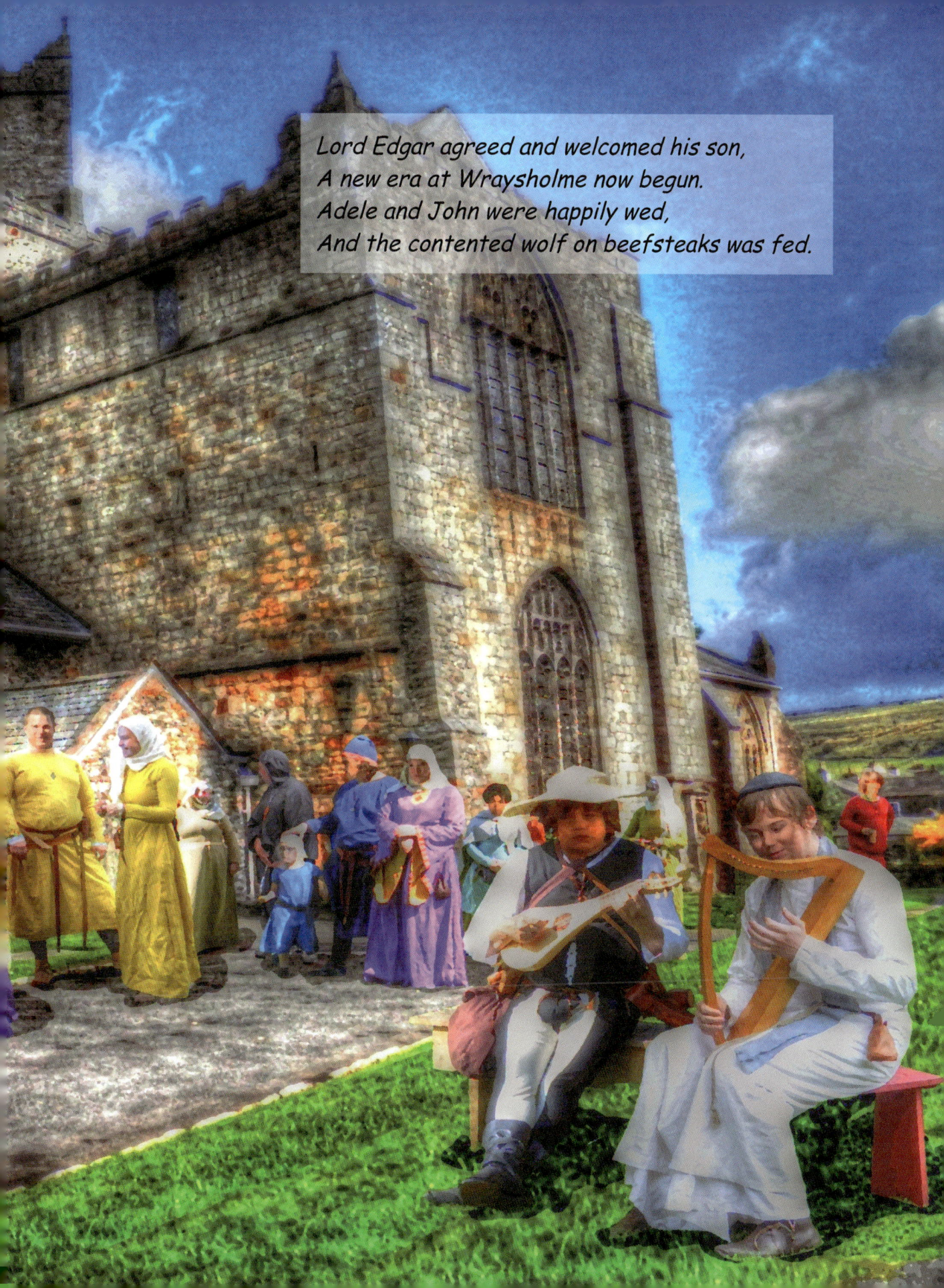

Lord Edgar agreed and welcomed his son,
A new era at Wraysholme now begun.
Adele and John were happily wed,
And the contented wolf on beefsteaks was fed.

Their obedient wolf was no trouble at all,
The couple built their home at Holker Hall,
And so you see, like a wise old sage,
The wolf was not killed, but died of OLD AGE.

Samak Fishing in Yemen

Andrew Musgrave

The book your teachers WON'T want you to read

School Anarchy

(Bad, BAD, Children)

Chris Greave

Lightship

Guides & Publications

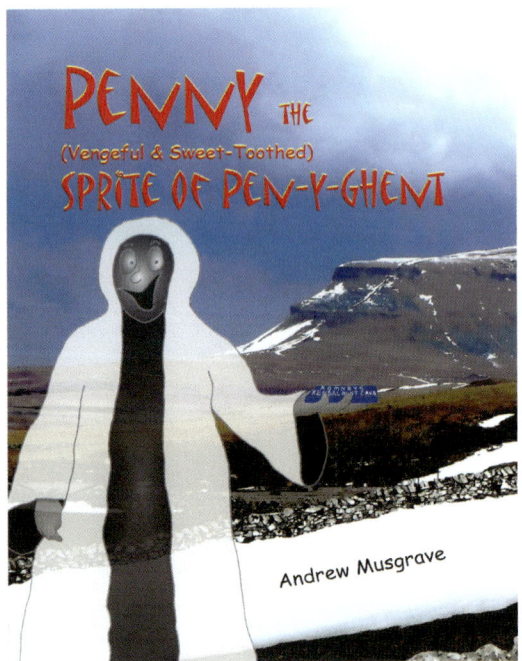

PENNY THE
(Vengeful & Sweet-Toothed)
SPRITE OF PEN-Y-GHENT

Andrew Musgrave

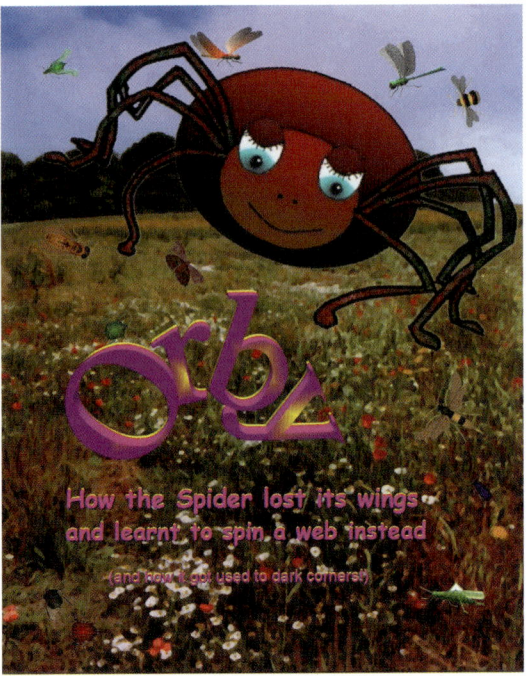

Orbz

How the Spider lost its wings
and learnt to spin a web instead

(and how it got used to dark corners)

Printed in Great Britain
by Amazon